Alfie Gets in First

Other Picture Books by
SHIRLEY HUGHES
Alfie's Feet
Alfie Gives a Hand
An Evening at Alfie's
The Big Alfie and Anne Rose Storybook
Dogger
(Winner of the 1977 Kate Greenaway Medal)
Helpers
(Highly commended for the 1975 Kate Greenaway
Medal and Winner of the 1976 Other Award)
Moving Molly
Sally's Secret
The Trouble with Jack
Up and Up

For
Jamie and Henry

British Library Cataloguing in Publication Data is available

ISBN 0–370–30417–9

Copyright © Shirley Hughes 1981
First published in 1981 by
The Bodley Head Children's Books
an imprint of Random House UK Ltd
20 Vauxhall Bridge Road, London SW1V 2SA

Reprinted 1982, 1984, 1985, 1994

Printed and bound in Belgium by
Proost International Book Production

Random House UK Limited Reg. No. 954009

Alfie Gets in First

Shirley Hughes

THE BODLEY HEAD

London

One day Alfie and Mum and Annie Rose were
coming home from the shops. Alfie ran on ahead
because he wanted to get home first. He ran all the
way from the corner to the front gate and up the
steps to the front door.

Then he sat down on the top step and waited for the others. Along came Mum, pushing Annie Rose and the shopping.

"I raced you!" called Alfie. "I'm back first, so there!"

Annie Rose didn't care. She was tired. She sat back in her push-chair and sucked her thumb.

Mum put the brake on the push-chair and left Annie Rose at the bottom of the steps while she lifted the basket of shopping up to the top. Then she found the key and opened the front door. Alfie dashed in ahead of her.

"I've won, I've won!" he shouted.

Mum put the shopping down in the hall and went back down the steps to lift Annie Rose out of her push-chair. But what do you think Alfie did then?

He gave the door a great big slam – BANG!
– just like that.

Then Mum was outside the door, holding
Annie Rose, and Alfie was inside with the
shopping. Mum's key was inside too.

"Open the door, Alfie," said Mum.

But Alfie didn't know how to open the door from the inside. The catch was too high up. Mum looked into the letter-box.

"Try to reach the catch and turn it," she said. Alfie tried but he couldn't quite reach it.

"Can you put the key through the letter-box?" said Mum. But Alfie couldn't reach the letter-box either.

Annie Rose was hungry as well as tired. She began to cry. Then Alfie began to cry too. He didn't like being all by himself on the wrong side of the door. Just then Mrs MacNally came hurrying across the street to see what all the noise was about.

She and Mum took it in turns to say
encouraging things into the letter-box.
But Alfie still couldn't open the door.

"Go and fetch your little chair from the sitting-room and then you'll be able to reach the catch," said Mum. But Alfie didn't try to fetch his little chair. He just went on crying, louder and louder, and Annie Rose cried louder and louder too.

"There's my Maureen," said Mrs MacNally. "I'm sure she'll be able to help."

Mrs MacNally's Maureen was a big girl. Right away she came and joined Mum and Annie Rose and Mrs MacNally on the top step.

"Mmm, might have to break a window," she said. "But I'll try to climb up the drain-pipe first, if you like."

But Mrs MacNally didn't like that idea at all.

"Oh no, Maureen, you might hurt yourself," she said.

Just then Alfie's very good friend the milkman came up the street in his milk-float.

When he saw Mum and Annie Rose and Mrs MacNally
and Mrs MacNally's Maureen all standing on the top
step he stopped his float and said:

"What's the trouble?"

So they told him.

"Don't worry, mate," the milkman shouted. "We'll
soon have you out of there."

"Mmm, looks as though this lock's going to be difficult to break," said the milkman. But then Mrs MacNally's Maureen had a very good idea. She ran to ask the window-cleaner, who was working up the street, if he would bring his ladder and climb up to the bathroom window. And, of course, when the window-cleaner heard about Alfie he came hurrying along with his ladder as quickly as he could.

Then Mum and Annie Rose and Mrs MacNally and
Mrs MacNally's Maureen and the milkman all stood on
the top step and watched while the window-cleaner put
his ladder up against the house. He started to climb
up to the bathroom window. But when he was half-way
up the ladder, what do you think happened?

The front door suddenly opened and there was Alfie! He had managed to reach the catch and turn it – like that – after all.

He was *very* pleased with himself. He opened the front door as wide as it would go and stood back grandly to let everybody in.

Then the window-cleaner came down from his
ladder, and he and the milkman and Mrs MacNally's
Maureen and Mrs MacNally and Annie Rose and Mum
and Alfie all went into the kitchen and had tea together.